Copyright © 1997 by Nord-Süd Verlag AG, Gossau Zürich, Switzerland.
First published in Switzerland under the title *Rapunzel*.
English translation copyright © 1997 by North-South Books Inc.

First published in the United States, Great Britain, Canada,
Australia, and New Zealand in 1997 by North-South Books,
an imprint of Nord-Süd Verlag AG, Gossau Zürich, Switzerland.
Distributed in the United States by North-South Books Inc., New York.
First paperback edition published in 2000 by North-South Books.

Library of Congress Cataloging-in-Publication Data
Rapunzel. English
Rapunzel : a fairy tale / [collected] by Jacob & Wilhelm Grimm ;
illustrated by Maja Dusíková ; translated by Anthea Bell.
Summary: A retelling of the traditional tale in which a beautiful
girl with long golden hair is imprisoned in a lonely tower by a witch.
[1. Fairy tales. 2. Folklore—Germany.] I. Grimm, Jacob,
1785-1863. II. Grimm, Wilhelm, 1786-1859. III. Dusíková, Maja,
ill. IV. Bell, Anthea. V. Title.
PZ8.R1866   1997
398.22—dc21
[E]   96-44816
A CIP catalogue record for this book is available
from The British Library.
ISBN 1-55858-684-9 (trade binding)
1 3 5 7 9 TB 10 8 6 4 2
ISBN 1-55858-685-7 (library binding)
1 3 5 7 9 LB 10 8 6 4 2
ISBN 0-7358-1304-3 (paperback)
1 3 5 7 9 PB 10 8 6 4 2
Printed in Belgium

For more information about our books, and the authors and artists
who create them, visit our web site: www.northsouth.com

Rapunzel

A FAIRY TALE BY

Jacob & Wilhelm Grimm

ILLUSTRATED BY

Maja Dusíková

TRANSLATED BY

Anthea Bell

North-South Books

NEW YORK · LONDON

ONCE UPON A TIME there were a man and a woman who had wanted a child for a very long time, but in vain. At last, however, the woman believed the good Lord was going to grant her wish.

From her house she could see into a lovely garden full of the most beautiful flowers and delicious herbs, but no one ever dared go into that garden, because it belonged to a powerful witch.

One day the woman stood at her window looking down into the garden, and she saw a bed where the salad herb called rampion or rapunzel grew. The woman felt a great longing to eat some of those herbs. She wanted them more and more every day, but since she could not get any rapunzel from the garden, she became weak, and pale, and miserable. Her husband was alarmed.

"What is the matter, dear wife?" he asked.

"Oh," she said, "I'll die if I can't have some of that rapunzel to eat!"

Her husband, who loved her dearly, said to himself: You can't let your wife die! You must get her some of those herbs at any price!

So when twilight fell that evening, he climbed over the wall into the witch's garden, hastily picked a handful of rapunzel, and brought it home to his wife.

She made it into a salad at once, and ate it greedily. However, she had enjoyed the rapunzel so much that the next day she wanted it three times as much as before, and she asked her husband to climb over the wall into the witch's garden again.

So when twilight fell he climbed over the wall once more, but when he was down in the garden he had a dreadful scare, for he saw the witch herself there in front of him.

"How dare you climb into my garden like a thief and steal my rapunzel!" she said angrily. "You'll be sorry for this!"

"Oh, please have mercy!" begged the man. "I did it only out of desperation: My wife saw your rapunzel from the window, and longed for it so much that she said she would die if she didn't have some to eat."

At that the witch relented slightly and said, "Very well, you can have as much of my rapunzel as you like, but on one condition. You must give me the baby your wife is about to bear. It will be well looked after. I will care for it like a mother."

In his fear the man agreed to everything, and as soon as his wife had her baby, the witch appeared, gave the little girl the name of Rapunzel, and carried her off.

Rapunzel grew into the loveliest child under the sun. When she was twelve years old, however, the witch shut her up in a tower that stood in the middle of the forest and had neither stairs nor a door. When the witch wanted to get in, she would stand at the foot of the tower and call: *"Rapunzel, Rapunzel, let down your hair."*

Rapunzel had beautiful long hair, as fine as spun gold, and as soon as she heard the witch's voice, she would take the long braid and wind it around a hook by the window. Then her hair fell down and down, all the way down to the ground, and the witch climbed up it.

One day the king's son happened to be riding through the forest, and as he passed the tower he heard a song, such a beautiful song that he stopped to listen. It was Rapunzel, singing sweetly to pass the time in her lonely tower.

The prince wanted to climb up to her, and looked for a doorway into the tower, but there was no door to be found.

He rode home, but the song had moved his heart so much that he went back to the forest every day to hear it.

One day, when he was standing behind a tree, he saw the witch come along and heard her call: *"Rapunzel, Rapunzel, let down your hair."*

Then Rapunzel let her braid of hair down, and the witch climbed up to her.

If that's the ladder leading up into the tower, thought the prince, then I'll try it myself.

The next day, when dusk was falling, the prince went to the tower and called: "*Rapunzel, Rapunzel, let down your hair.*"

Rapunzel let her hair down at once, and the king's son climbed up it.

At first Rapunzel was alarmed to see the king's son come in, for she had never set eyes on a man before. However, the prince began talking gently to her, telling her that his heart had been so moved by her singing that he could not rest until he saw her for himself.

Then Rapunzel forgot her fears, and when he asked if she would marry him, she said yes, and put her hand in his.

"I will go with you gladly," she said, "but it will be difficult for me to get down from this tower. Every time you come to see me, you must bring me a silken cord. I'll weave a ladder out of the cords, and when it's ready I will climb down and you can carry me off on your horse."

They agreed that the prince would visit her every evening until the ladder was ready, for the old witch came in the daytime.

The witch noticed nothing until one day, without thinking, Rapunzel asked her, "Tell me, Godmother, how is it that you seem so much heavier than the young prince when you climb up?"

"Oh, you wicked child!" cried the witch. "What's all this? I thought I'd shut you safely away from the whole world, but you've tricked me!"

In her fury, she seized Rapunzel's lovely hair and *snip, snap*, cut it all off. There lay the beautiful braid on the floor. The witch had no pity on poor Rapunzel, but took her to live alone in a deserted part of the forest.

That very evening the witch fastened the braid of hair she had cut off to the hook by the window, and when the king's son came and called: *"Rapunzel, Rapunzel, let down your hair,"* she let the hair down.

The king's son climbed up. At the top of the tower, however, he found not his beloved Rapunzel but the witch, glaring at him with venomous rage.

"Aha," she said scornfully, "so you've come for your sweetheart, have you? Well, the pretty bird has flown and won't be singing anymore. The cat has caught her, and will soon scratch out your own eyes. Rapunzel is lost to you. You will never see her again."

The king's son was beside himself with grief, and in his despair he jumped out of the tower window. He was not killed, but he fell into some thorn bushes, and the thorns put out his eyes.

He wandered blindly through the forest, eating nothing but roots and berries, weeping and wailing for the loss of his beloved Rapunzel.

So he wandered the country for several years, until at last he came to the deserted place where Rapunzel was living in great grief and misery.

All at once he heard a voice, and it seemed to him very familiar. He went in the direction of that voice, and when he reached it Rapunzel recognized him. She flung her arms around his neck and wept. Two of her tears fell on his eyes, and suddenly he could see as well as ever.

He took Rapunzel home to his kingdom, where the people welcomed him back with joy, and Rapunzel and her prince lived happily ever after.